For Maria Silvia and Francesca,
who wanted a book like this – MH

For Lola, Lenny, Lucille and Babette – RA

JANETTA OTTER-BARRY BOOKS

First published in Great Britain and in the USA in 2014 by
Frances Lincoln Children's Books,
74-77 White Lion Street, London N1 9PF
www.franceslincoln.com

A CIP catalogue record for this book is available from the British Library.

ISBN 978-1-84780-592-8

Illustrated with watercolours

Set in Elroy

Printed in China

1 3 5 7 9 8 6 4 2

WELCOME
TO THE FAMILY

Written by **MARY HOFFMAN**

Illustrated by **ROS ASQUITH**

F

FRANCES LINCOLN
CHILDREN'S BOOKS

Look at all these people!

Some people think living
alone can be fun.

Others can get a bit
lonely on their own.

Some grown-ups prefer to live in groups of friends.

And some like to live with just one other person.

Two people who love each other
may want to have children,
to make a family.

And when the baby is born, she or he is usually very welcome.

Then there may be more.

Sometimes, if two people can't have a baby themselves,
they can adopt a baby or child. This means they find
a child who can't stay with their original family,
because their birth parents aren't able to look after them.

And when that happens, the baby or child
needs a new family that is right for them.

And it might just be one person who can provide a loving family.

An adopted child is just as welcome as any other child. And their new parents become their real mother or father.

Some babies and children can't stay with their birth parents all the time. They might need another family to look after them for a while, until their original parents can manage to have them back.

This other family is called their foster family and the children are very welcome.

Children are usually able to see their birth family while they are living with their foster parents.

In some countries, two mommies
or two daddies can make a family
by adopting or fostering children.

Sometimes, however much a couple love each other and want a family, a baby doesn't happen and then doctors can help.

You need two cells to make a baby – one from a man and one from a woman.

When a baby doesn't happen naturally,
doctors can help get the cells together.

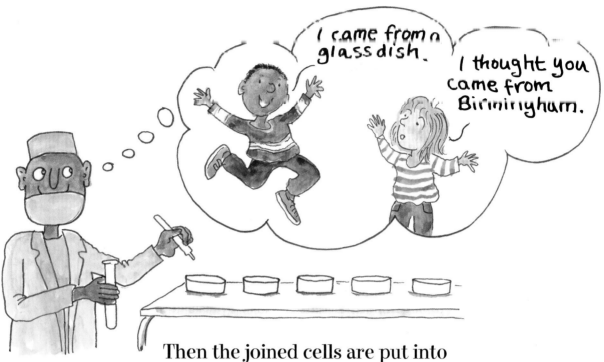

Then the joined cells are put into
the woman's tummy to grow,
just like any other baby. Millions of
babies have been made this way now.

When there are two mommies, they need
a male cell to make a baby with one of
their cells. They can get it from a friend,
or go to a special clinic for a male cell.

So is that your baby – or are you growing it for someone else?

When there are two daddies, they need a female cell, but they also need a woman to grow the baby in her body for them. This could be a friend, or someone they don't know.

My dads are finding a mommy to make another baby.

Then we'll have THREE children.

Sometimes a family can grow unexpectedly when a mommy or daddy finds a new partner who already has children. This is called 'blending' two families. But it's not like blending a milkshake; it doesn't always go smoothly.

It can take a while for the children to settle
down and get along together, and to get used
to a new person acting as their parent.
They can also worry about the mom or dad
who no longer lives with them.

Families are complicated. When they are unhappy, life can be very difficult, just because family members know each other so well. They know what will annoy you and what will get you into trouble with your parents.

But when families are happy, they are great.
The love between brothers and sisters
can last all their lives.

There has always been more than one way to make a family. Perhaps in the future there will be even more.

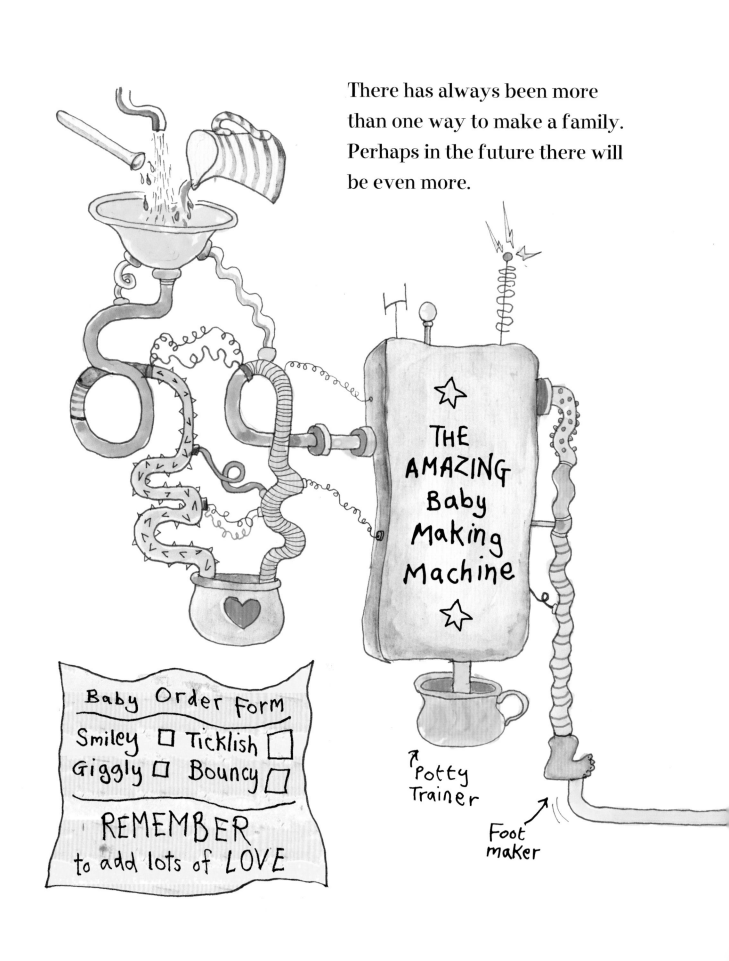

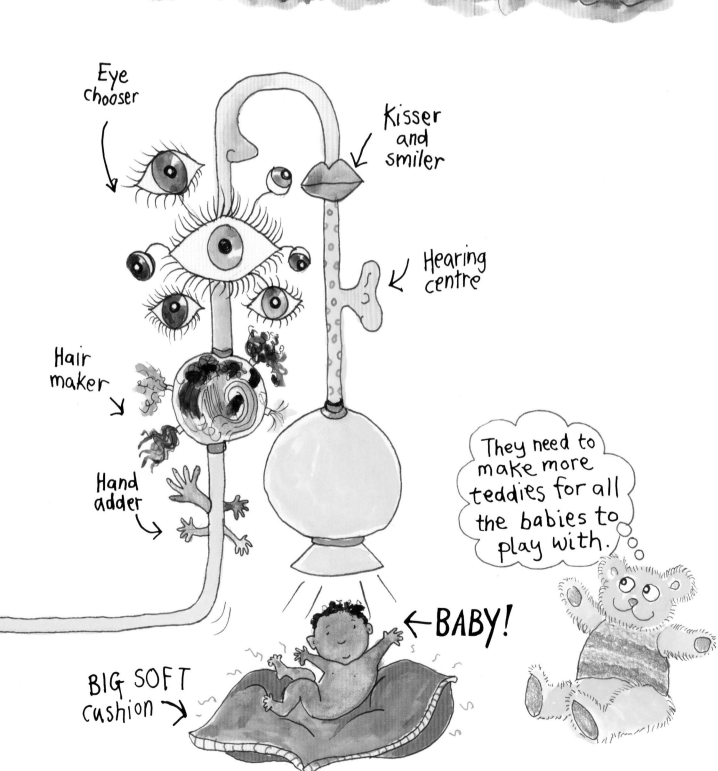

One thing is certain – there will always be new children and they will all need families. The important thing is feeling happy in the family you belong to.

Welcome to the family –

however you got there!

How did you come into YOUR family?